I dare you to climb over this steep and creepy hill.

Because over this steep and creepy hill . . .

there's an old, crumbly wall. And . . .

in this wall . . .

there's a looming, gloomy gate. And . . .

through this gate . . .

there's a mysterious, spooky church. And . . .

behind this church . . .

there's a dark and dreary graveyard. And . . .

in this graveyard . . .

there's an eerie, empty tomb. And I dare you
to look inside this tomb because inside
you will find a . . .